For Abbie and Alexis
—AMS

For Dad
—JG

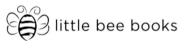 little bee books

A division of Bonnier Publishing Group
853 Broadway, New York, New York 10003
Text copyright © 2016 by Ann Marie Stephens
Illustrations copyright © 2016 by Jess Golden
All rights reserved, including the right of reproduction in whole
or in part in any form. LITTLE BEE BOOKS is a trademark of
Bonnier Publishing Group, and associated colophon is a
trademark of Bonnier Publishing Group.
Manufactured in China   LEO 1215
First Edition   10 9 8 7 6 5 4 3 2 1
Library of Congress Cataloging-in-Publication Data is available upon request.
ISBN 978-1-4998-0143-9

littlebeebooks.com
bonnierpublishing.com

SCUBA DOG

by **Ann Marie Stephens**   illustrated by **Jess Golden**

little bee books

This dog likes the ocean.

These dogs don't.

He swims.

They jam.

Different dogs.

While they make music, this dog sails his boat, past jumping waves.

He holds his breath and bobs with the moon jellies.

All of a sudden—

Could she be a new friend?
She likes the ocean too.

He is up.

She is down.

They meet in the middle.
1-2-3-Go!

But not for long.

He floats here and wags.

She floats there
and sings.

He sends her a shell.

She sends him one more bubble.

Faraway friends... for now.

**Back on land,
this dog dreams.**

He draws.

He has an idea.

Off to the dive shop!

Hit the books,

and the pool.

Pass the tests.
Get the gear.

Air in. Bubbles out.

Hello,
Scuba Dog!

Up and over, around and through. Off to find his friend.

Sometimes friends don't
need words.

They spin,

whirl,

and dive.

But not for long.
This whale needs to
find some food!

Scuba Dog begs her to stay a little longer.

He whips up a gift.

SWISH! Full steam ahead.

She leaves him with a song.
Goodbye, friend.

Back on land,
he plans a special hello.

He remembers
her song.

He hums it.
They strum it.

He taps it.
They rap it.

He takes seashells and sea glass,
and blends them like this.

He finds flip-flops and feathers,
and joins them like that.

Days come. Days go.
Scuba Dog hasn't made his hello.

Until...

Scuba Dog gives his gift...

...and gets one in return.

Sometimes friends don't need words.